RAYMOND PAUL BOYD

WAG
AND NOAH'S ARK

To order additional copies of this book, contact:
Xlibris
844-714-8691
www.Xlibris.com
Orders@Xlibris.com

ISBN: 978-1-6698-4928-5 (sc)
ISBN: 978-1-6698-4927-8 (e)

Print information available on the last page

Rev. date: 02/27/2023

Acknowledgment

As I begin to write, I sense, as always, the presence of my wife, Gloria (September 10, 1934–August 18, 2000), inspiring my imagination into a world of fantasy.

Prologue

A long, long time ago, there was a torrential of rain that fell on the earth for forty days and nights, causing all living things on earth to drown. The highest mountains were underwater; only those people in the ark that Noah had built with his sons and their wives were saved. The ark also held hundreds of pairs of animals and thirty pairs of flying creatures. One hundred and ninety days would elapse before all were able to leave the safety of the ark. Biblical scholars have pondered how there could have been enough food and water for all those in the ark. They also considered what became of those who has been left to drown. This narrative seeks to answer all these questions.

Two doves raised a large blue flag. One held the right side, and the other held the left side high above. In the heavenly animal kingdom, all who saw it knew they were to come to the great hall. The flag was a summons to hear what the all-knowing Bow-wow had to say.

When Bow-wow saw that all had arrived in the great hall, he said, "I would like you all to know that our brother Wag is once again a comforter due to his good works in the world of humankind, where so many of our sisters and brothers live. Now, if Brother Wag would kindly come up on stage, I will present him with the golden doggy bone of merit, attached to an unbreakable blue-and-silver ribbon."

Wag said, "Thank you, Bow-wow; I shall wear it with pride."

Bow-wow then asked, "Would you like to hear the story of Brother Wag's first assignment, which many of you here have witnessed?"

There was thunderous applause.

To the delight of all in the heavenly kingdom, Bow—wow began to tell the story.

This is a story of the earth, during a time when all who lived on it perished, with the exception of those who were in the ark constructed by Noah and his three sons. After the ark had been built, only some of our sisters and brothers were selected to enter.

Black clouds that had never before been seen hovered over the African plains. All our sisters and brothers instinctively gathered at the site where Noah had constructed the ark. There was discontent about which animals would be selected to enter the lifesaving ark. Suddenly two of every kind of animal, male and female, and also the same of the fowl of the air went into the ark. The others watched in silence.

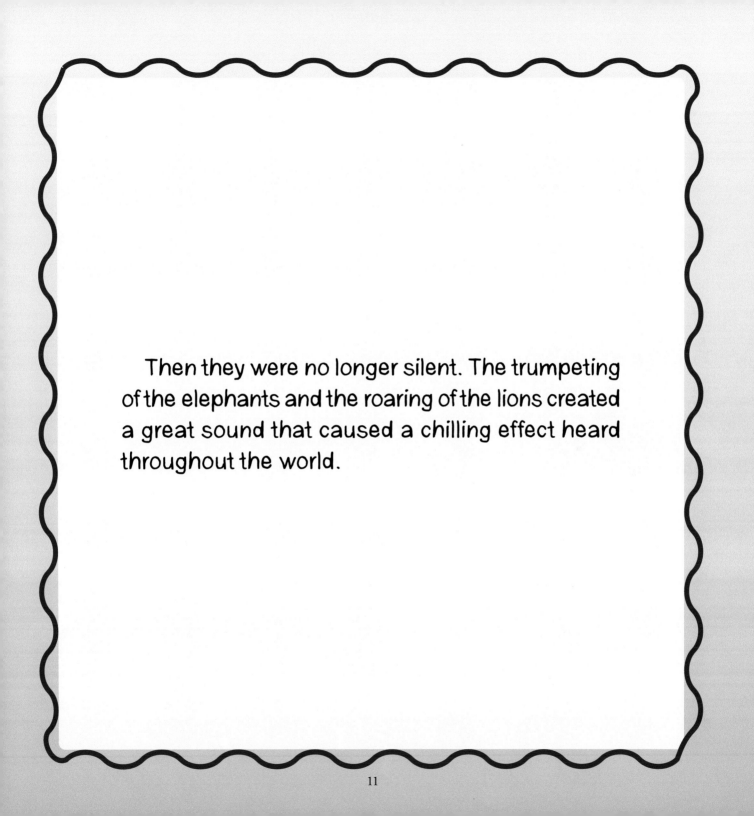

Then they were no longer silent. The trumpeting of the elephants and the roaring of the lions created a great sound that caused a chilling effect heard throughout the world.

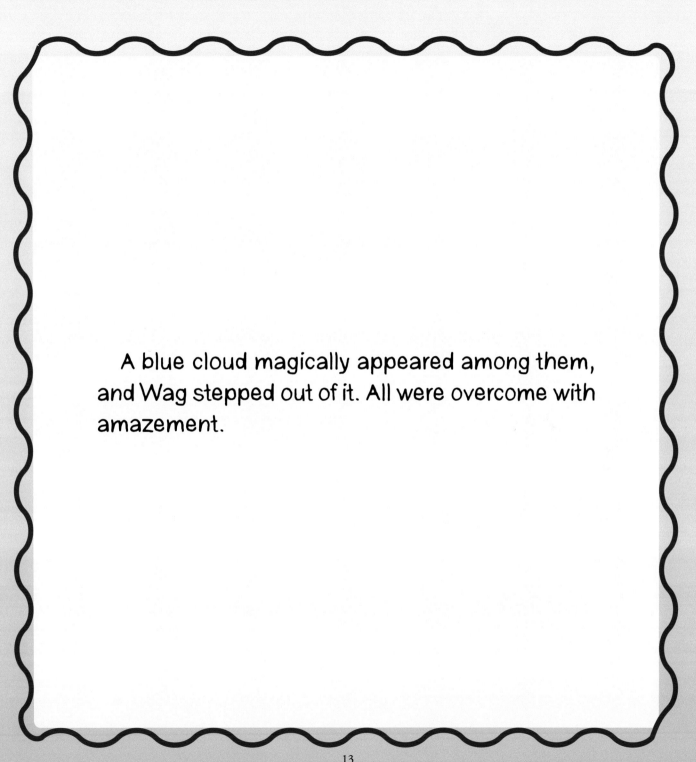

A blue cloud magically appeared among them, and Wag stepped out of it. All were overcome with amazement.

The hyena was the first to speak. "Who are you? Have you come to drown with us?"

"I see you have been given knowledge of your fate, said Wag, "but I have come to give you all words of comfort that shall rid you of your fears. Please listen to what I have come to say."

They all answered, "We don't need words of comfort."

"We shall see," replied Wag.

"I do not need words of comfort," said the great big bald eagle. "My kind and I shall fly up to the highest mountain and wait until the rain stops. What do you have to say to that?"

Wag did not reply.

The giraffe spoke next. "I have nothing to fear, as the water cannot reach my mouth. When my kind and I stand on top of a hill, our long legs and long necks shall prevent us from drowning. What do you have to say to that?"

Wag did not respond.

The cheetah spoke next and said, "I am so swift of foot that I can outrun the floodwaters. Just watch me and my kind run. What do you have to say to that?"

Wag did not respond.

Next to speak was the hippopotamus, who said, "I am not tall or able to fly, but I cannot drown. I can stay underwater for a long, long time, and so can all my kind. Do you have anything to say to that, Brother Wag?"

Wag did not reply.

The zebra said, "I also am swift of foot. Although my kind and I cannot fly or stay underwater, we can outrun the coming waters. As for your words of comfort, I don't believe they can add to how fast we can run."

Wag smiled but did not comment.

The mighty elephant said, "My kind and I are the largest in the animal kingdom, and we can survive storms as we have always done. Do you think I am wrong?"

Wag didn't reply.

The monkey, who had been waiting to speak, jumped up on the back of the elephant and said, "I am not worried. It's true that my kind and I cannot linger underwater or fly, but we can ride on the back on these great big elephants. What do you think of that?"

Wag smiled but did not answer.

The lion spoke next and said sadly, "My kind and I cannot do anything like the others can; even though I am the king of the jungle, we cannot save ourselves. So we are anxious for your words of comfort."

Wag smiled and didn't reply.

Next, the ostrich stepped forward and said, "My kind and I can use our extremely long legs to take us to safety. Therefore, we have nothing to fear. Have we?"

Wag gave no reply.

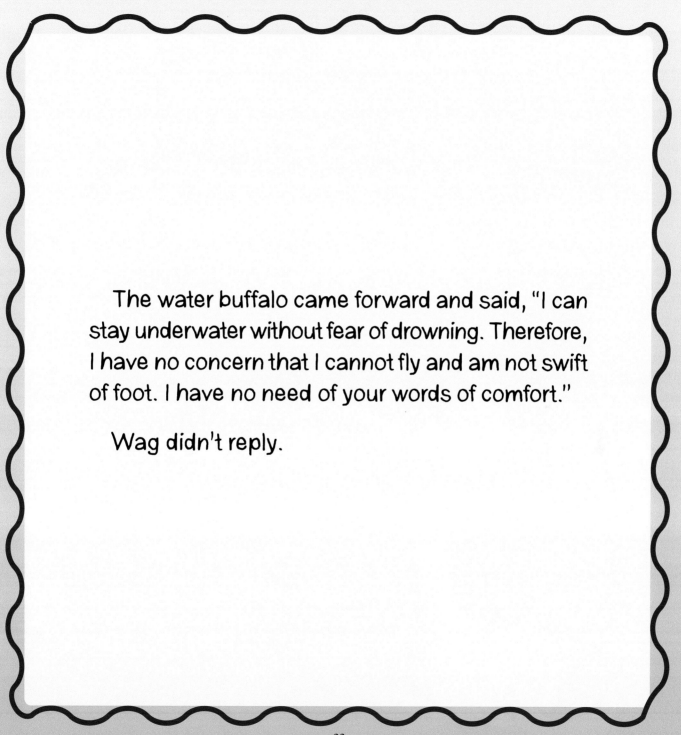

The water buffalo came forward and said, "I can stay underwater without fear of drowning. Therefore, I have no concern that I cannot fly and am not swift of foot. I have no need of your words of comfort."

Wag didn't reply.

Wag then listened to the crocodile, who happily explained why he and his kind had no fear of the coming storm. Unlike the others that could fly or were swift of foot, he and his kind could eat and sleep underwater for that was their domain.

Wag made no comment.

Wag then listened to what the gorilla had to say. He spoke with confidence saying, "My kind and I do not have the ability to fly, and we are not swift of foot. But we have great strength and can climb to the top of the highest mountain for safety. What do you think of that?"

Wag didn't reply.

Wag then listened to the great horned owl as he said, "Unlike the others, my kind and I do not seek safety, as we know there is no place on earth to go. Therefore, we know it is wise to hear words of comfort from him who I believe has come from the spirit world."

"Thank you," Wag replied.

Wag decided to give his words of comfort to the bald eagle and explained that even if he and his kind perched atop the highest mountain, the rain would fall from the sky until all the mountains in the world were underwater. "But be assured that the moment before drowning, you all shall enter the heavenly kingdom of animals," said Wag.

Wag then addressed all who had spoken to him about how they planned to avoid being drown. He told them it was fruitless. Even though the water buffalo, hippopotamus, and crocodile could stay underwater for a long time, they still must breathe. But they would find there would be no air to breathe. "But have no fear, as you will all enter the heavenly animal kingdom. I shall see you all there," said Wag.

All the animals huddled together, feeling a sense of contentment. Black clouds hovered ominously over the African plains. Then suddenly several bolts of lightning piercing the clouds, causing a torrential rain that began to flood the earth.

The massive door of the ark slowly begun to close, but before it could, Wag entered the ark unobserved. The raging waters raised the ark soon, causing for it to float above the ocean of water. The animals begun to talk among themselves: "How long shall it be before the rain stops?"

"I can tell you when it will stop, sisters and brothers. My name is Wag, and I have come to comfort you and to tell you the rain will end in forty days. One hundred fifty days after that, you will be able leave the safety of the ark."

Mrs. Owl said, "May I ask a question?"

"Yes, please do," replied Wag.

"Thank you, Brother. If we are to remain for the length of time you have stated, we all can see there isn't food and water enough to feed us for the many days. How will we eat?"

Wag replied, "Be assured there is enough food for forty days. Be of good cheer, and afterward you all shall sleep until the door of the ark is open."

Bow—wow concluded his tale and asked if everyone had enjoyed the story. There was a rousing yes. And then the owl asked, "But why was the earth flooded?"

Bow—wow said sadly, "The misbehavior of humankind."

The chatter of all in the great hall stopped by the appearance of St. Francis, formerly of Assisi, France; his saintly appearance included a dazzling white robe and a golden halo hovering above his partially shaved pate. A multitude of blue and yellow canaries flew together, suspended in midair, with two archangels. One was Michael, who stood on the right side of the choir of birds, and the other was Gabriel, who stood on the left. They were there to vocalize. Saint Francis had selected "Amazing Grace" to conduct, and the sound of the choir was heavenly, something that all in God's kingdom enjoyed.

THE END?

Printed in the United States
by Baker & Taylor Publisher Services